The Wall Friends Club

First published in 2025 by HarperCollins *Children's Books*
An imprint of HarperCollins *Publishers* India
4th Floor, Tower A, Building No. 10, DLF Cyber City,
DLF Phase II, Gurugram, Haryana – 122002

2 4 6 8 10 9 7 5 3 1

Text © Varsha Seshan 2025
Illustrations © HarperCollins *Publishers* India 2025

P-ISBN: 978-93-6569-221-1
E-ISBN: 978-93-6569-359-1

Varsha Seshan asserts the moral right
to be identified as the author of this work.

This is a work of fiction and all characters and incidents described in this book are the product of the author's imagination. Any resemblance to actual persons, living or dead, is entirely coincidental.

All rights reserved. No part of this publication may be reproduced, stored in a retrieval system, or transmitted, in any form or by any means, electronic, mechanical, photocopying, recording or otherwise, without the prior permission of the publishers.

Cover design and art by Denise Antao
Inside illustrations by Denise Antao

Typeset in 12/14.3 PF Reminder at
HarperCollins *Publishers* India

Printed and bound at
Thomson Press (India) Ltd

This book is produced from independently certified FSC® paper
to ensure responsible forest management.

The Wall Friends Club

Varsha Seshan

Illustrated by
Denise Antao

HCCB
HARPERCOLLINS
CHILDREN'S BOOKS

The Wall Friends Club

11 June

~~Dear~~

Hi!

~~I am An someone who.~~

I don't know how to write this letter because I'm not supposed to talk to strangers. Most importantly, I must not tell strangers my name and address. I have no idea what the rules are about writing to strangers. Should be the same, right? But what about pen pals? My father had a pen pal ~~and.~~

Sorry. I'm a chatterbox. I am a writerbox too, hehe! But why a box? I wonder. If my friend V ever had a question like that, she would just Google it. ~~I'm~~ I don't do that! ☹

Hmm. I don't know how to write to a wall.

I read a book about someone putting things into the hollow of a tree and someone else finding them. ~~The book wasn't really about that, but~~ I don't r-e-a-l-l-y know what the hollow of a tree is, but I think I would be too scared to put my hand in. What if a snake lives inside? Or a bat! Do bats bite? Do snakes live in holes in trees? ~~You know, when I start imagining~~

But the gap in this wall is perfect. It's funny, right? For days, I didn't even notice it. And then, when I saw it today, I thought, aha! I must put something here! Something small and fun. A sweet? A sticker? But what's the point, if I have no idea if anyone found it, right? And then I thought, ooh! A letter. Then maybe, just maybe, someone will reply.

So, that's what this is about.

The Wall Friends Club

I might be writing to no one. Maybe tomorrow, or next week, I'll come back and find my letter sitting there and staring back at me. Or worse, I'll find wet mush that no one can ever read.

But I hope, hope, hope someone finds it and writes back. That will be the coolest thing ever.

Okay, that's all. I don't know what else to say.

~~Love Regards~~

~~Yours~~

Bye!

13 June

Hello An---!! (Hehehe!)

It was So Exciting to find your letter!!

I walk home from school through this park every day, and I thought the little paper stuck in the wall would be a pamphlet or something. I collect pamphlets to write stuff at the back (like this letter!). (I love brackets!)

So I took it out — and ... Best Thing Ever. What a super idea! I didn't want anyone to ask me what I was reading, so I hid behind the wall and read it secretly. Then I hunted everywhere to find a place to write my reply secretly. And on my way to school tomorrow, I'll slip it into the wall (secretly).

So, your wish came true! Someone DID find your

The Wall Friends Club

letter, and that someone IS writing back!

Are we friends yet, or are we still strangers?

Let's play a game! I know that the first two letters of your name are 'An' (you can call me Detective), so I'll tell you the first two letters of mine. I'm Sr. When I feel I know you better, I'll tell you the next letter.

Is it safe to tell you how old I am? Ten. You? (Why would it be unsafe to tell someone how old I am?)

I've been sitting here for I don't know how long wondering what else to write. I want to fill this page. What's the point of wasting blank paper? (Even if this is the back of an old political thingy that someone came and gave everyone in our area. I collected everyone's pamphlets. I don't know who the Moustache Man is, but paper is always useful. To practise sums, spelling ... and now to write to you! Don't know where to close the bracket. So I'll do it here.) Open brackets that never close are the most annoying things in the world!

It looks like I'm as much of a writerbox as you. I didn't know that about me! So, after everything, this is what I thought of sharing.

The Wall Friends Club

Things I like	Things I Don't like
1. New clothes	1. Dirty jokes (please tell me you don't like them either)
2. Holidays	2. Wet socks
3. Brinjal (yes, really, but nobody in my school likes it)	3. ~~Ur~~ One girl in my school (I hate scratching stuff out. It's such a waste of paper.)

Oops. Sorry, sorry, sorry. I just realized. You do scratch out stuff.

It's fine, okay? I don't want to be mean. I'm sorry. I hate judge-y people. I'm not judge-y, promise! How soon can I expect a reply? Can I send love yet?

Bye!

---

15 June

Dear Detective Sr,

Your letter made me SO happy!

I'm almost ten years old too. ~~It would have been So Wierd Bizzarre~~ I was trying so hard not to scratch anything out, but it's so difficult. And I don't know how to spell these words. I'm just going to write wierd even though that spelling looks bizzarre.

I know, I know, I should just look up the spellings. V keeps telling

The Wall Friends Club

me that. But I HATE getting up in the middle of something to look up a word. Do you always look words up?

I forgot what I was writing, so I had to go back and look! Anyway. It would have been so EWWW if an old uncle had found my letter and written to me.

I don't know if we're friends yet, but friends need to know a lot about each other, so here you go.

Things I like	Things I Don't like
1. Reading	1. BRINJAL!
2. Cycling	2. Dirty jokes (Yay!) (I used brackets too, just like Detective Sr!)
3. Writing letters and poems	3. Milk
4. Singing in the bathroom	4. Injections

When is your birthday? Mine is on the 31st of August. It's AGES away. I'll be ten, so it's a special birthday because unless I live to be 100, I'll be in double digits for the REST OF MY LIFE.

ME!

The Wall Friends Club

Do you have any brothers or sisters? I don't.
I'm not sure if my parents would allow me to leave a photograph in a public place, so I cut my face out and put a dog's face instead. I don't liiiiikkke dogs, but I love puppies!

Bye!

P.S. It's so cool to write on the back of pamphlets! Children will save the world!

---

16 June

Hello, Anxxxx, you look so funny with a dog's face! I can't help imagining you like that now, sticking out your tongue and writing letters. I don't have a picture of me, so here's a picture of Elsa. I found it on the classroom floor! Isn't she pretty? (I asked everyone, of course, if the picture was theirs, but it was no one's.) I love Elsa! She is my favourite EVERYTHING. My favourite character,

The Wall Friends Club

my favourite cartoon, she wears my favourite clothes, she has my favourite eye colour... Like I said, my favourite everything.

I'm going to tell you the next letter of my name. It's i. Any guesses?

My birthday is on the 12th of February, so I'm 6 months and 19 days older than you. You're so funny, Anxxxx! I never thought about the double-digit thing!

Yes, I have a sister. Sometimes, she's ugh-so-irritating and sometimes she's my best friend (usually the first). She is 13 and she studies All The Time. The worst thing is that teachers in school keep calling me ~~Kr~~'s sister, or worse, calling me by her name.

You like writing poems! Yay! We have a poetry writing competition in school and I want to write a poem for it, but it has to be something DIFFERENT. I don't think I'm very good at writing poems, but I want to try! Please, please, please let's write something together?

I'm already hoping you'll say yes, so here's my first line:

Urja has a secret. That is nothing new.

Your turn!

So that no random uncle or aunty finds my letter, I'm going to tuck it deep in. Time to go home! I'm

The Wall Friends Club

sure my mother is going to ask me how come I get home so late nowadays. The good thing is that my sister goes for a special coaching class after school, so we don't walk home together. (She even got a scholarship for it, you know? Even if she's very irritating, we're all super-proud of her.) Otherwise, how would I ever have managed to write to you?

Sri

P.S. I have a dictionary with me all the time and I usually look things up like your friend V because I'm always afraid people will laugh at me if I spell things incorrectly. I wish I was like you! Bindaas! (I almost didn't write that word because my teacher keeps telling us to use language carefully and not mix languages. But I wanted to do something brave.) (Okay, maybe it's not <u>that</u> brave, but now I have no more paper left. Bye!)

18 June

Dear Sri (shti? ja? vidya? Lanka? It's a joke, okay? Please don't get upset!),

Also, look, look, I'm using more brackets just like you! But I'm scared I'll forget to close them one day, and then you'll be so angry! Hehe.

For just a minute, I thought you had not written to me because your letter was innnnnside! I was a teeny tiny bit afraid pulling it out. I haven't told ANYONE this, not even my best friend because I feel she'll make fun of me, but I'm scared of lizards. What if I put my hand

The Wall Friends Club

in and ewwwwww! Ew, ew, ew!

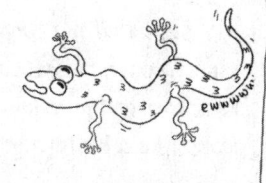

I'm leaving my favourite sharpener here for you too, with my letter. We're friends now, right? So it's for you.

If your sister goes for a special class after school, how come you can't go home and write in your room? Also, your sister must be So Smart to get a scholarship! Do your parents keep coming into your room? I have a friend like that. If she shuts her door, her parents open it imMidiatly. When we're playing in her room, her mother comes in EVERY TEN MINUTES!

Writing a poem together is such a super-duper idea, Sri! Here you go.

**Urja has a secret. That is nothing new.
Ana found out what it was, so now she knows it too.**

There you go, Detective Sri! You have the next letter of my name. Any guesses?

Just wondering—is Urja a real person?

Yesterday, I decorated my room with dolphin posters. Dolphins are my favourite animal. They look like they're always smiling.

The Wall Friends Club

V says that my room looks like a ~~kindergarden kintergarden~~ kintergarten classroom, but I think she's jealous. In her room, she has a red chair and a yellow table, so you tell me. Whose room do you think looks like a kintergarten classroom, huh?

Love,
Ana

My room looks awesome. Will you come home someday and see it?

P.S. I never thought of it as brave to spell a word incorrectly. Ha! I love it. When V makes fun of my spelling, I'll just tell her I'm brave and creative. Thank you, Sri!

---

20 June

Dear Ana (nya? ndita? hita? conda? Joking!)

Your guesses were all wrong! How about one of mine? But I love Sri Lanka! I'm going to sign off as Sri Lanka. And since that's decided, I'll tell you my name. It's Sriya.

I'm so sorry, I totally forgot to tell you I can't write letters on weekends! I come through this park only on my way to and from school.

And now, I'm doing something I've never done before. I'm thrilled-terrified. Sshh! I picked up your letter on my way to school, and I was so, so happy to see that my super-serious bench partner was sitting with someone else today (because that girl's bench partner is absent). I'm all alone! So, I put your letter into my English textbook and read it in

The Wall Friends Club

class. Now, I'm writing when we're supposed to be doing Maths classwork! Hehe!

Yes, Urja is a real person. How did you know? She's the girl in my class whom I don't like (if you remember my list of things I don't like. She's not a thing, I know, but I HAD to put her on the list.). She ALWAYS has secrets, and she ALWAYS whispers them in front of me, just to make me feel left out. On her first day at school (she joined my school this year), she told my best friends I had lice. They didn't sit with me for lunch, and they didn't even tell me what happened. Sonia (one of my two best friends) told me after ONE WEEK why they weren't sitting with me anymore.

Now you understand the first line of the poem, don't you? I'm going on with it!

**Urja has a secret. That is nothing new.
Ana found out what it was, so now
she knows it too.
Ana then told Sriya, so Sriya's
not left out.**

I think you would tell me. Wouldn't you?

Thank you so much for the sharpener. ♡ No one has ever given me their favourite anything before. I'll keep it safe forever!

Love,
Sri Lanka

The Wall Friends Club

22 June

Hello Sri Lanka, I'm Anandi!

 Urja sounds like a horrible person. Why would she tell anyone you had lice? And I HATE people who whisper. It's so mean.

 I don't want you to feel bad, Sri Lanka, but I don't think your best friends were very nice either. If you had been my best friend, I would have come and told you that Urja said you had lice. Wouldn't you? Did they at least say they're sorry?

 I thought and thought about how to continue our poem, but you know what I realized? I don't like Urja, so I changed it.

> Veena has a secret that she
> shares with just a few.
> Ana found out what it was,
> so now she knows it too.
> Ana then told Sriya,
> so Sriya's not left out.
> Now everyone but Urja knows
> what the secret's all about!

Ha! And of course I would tell you my secret!

 Have you kept all my letters so far? I've kept yours safe, locked inside my personal diary, along with your pretty Elsa.

The Wall Friends Club

I've put a tiny sweet in with this letter. I hope the ants don't eat it first!

Please say you'll come home someday and see my dolphins.

Love,
Wall Friend
Anaconda

P.S. Oh, and the Veena in the poem is my best friend, the V who says my room looks like a KG classroom. I really, really want to tell her about you. May I?

---

24 June

Dear Wall Friend Anaconda,

I really want to come home and see your dolphins, but I love my letter-writing friend. Will I lose her if I meet her?

I had to clean your sweet a little (the ants HAD got to it first), but I ate it. It was the sweetest sweet I've ever eaten. Thank you, Anandi the Anaconda. You're so nice.

I love your poem! May I send it for the competition? We will win! I'm sure of it. I want to write your name also at the bottom, but I don't think that's allowed. But if we win, we'll share the prize, okay?

Sonia and Esha did say they were sorry, but... they're stuck to Urja like Fevicol, and I don't know why. All three are on the hockey team, so they eat quickly during break and then go and play. PLUS,

The Wall Friends Club

they take the same school bus home, so I guess they have to be friends. I walk home alone because I live close to school. We didn't FIGHT-fight, so we are still friends, but I don't know if we're proper best friends anymore.

Would you mind keeping the WFs a secret for just a little longer? I've never had such a special secret before.

I made a bookmark for you! I hope you like it.

Oh-ho! It's starting to rain. I'll stop here.

Love,
A very rushed Sri Lanka who doesn't want to get wet (I hate wet socks, remember?)

P.S. Sorry, I'll put this letter in only on Monday!

---

27 June

Dear Sri Lanka,

Very, very quick letter because I'm going for a birthday party today. It's OUR poem! Submit it, please. We WILL win!

Love,
WFA

The Wall Friends Club

Hi,

I found a letter from WFA to Sri Lanka! That is SO WEIRD. Leaving the letter here, along with this note.

Did you make up names for yourselves?

Or wait, is this a silly game that only one person is playing?

Uh-oh. Sri, someone else found my letter. What should we do?

And Anonymiss Letter Writer, if you read this first, this note is for you. DON'T READ OUR PRIVATE LETTERS. This is Something Special between Sri Lanka and WFA. TRESSPASSERS NOT ~~ALOUD~~ ALLOWED.

You spelt trespassers wrong. Ha.

I just checked. You also spelt anonymous wrong. Double ha.

---

4 July

Dear WFA,

I wish we could talk about what to do next. Today, I FINALLY came up with a plan. I'm going to write another letter and put it somewhere else. And I'm going to tell you where that place is in code! Ready?

Write down your birthday and my birthday. Write the number also in words. For example, if my birthday is 13th September, write THIRTEEN

The Wall Friends Club

SEPTEMBER. Okay?

Now, here's the clue:

Word 1
Letter 1: The last letter of my birth month
Letter 2: The second letter of my birth month
Letter 3: The fourth letter of my birth date
Letter 4: Again, the fourth letter of my birth date
Letter 5: The seventh letter of your birth date
Letter 6: The second letter of my birth date

Word 2
Letter 1: The fifth letter of your birth month
Letter 2: The third letter of my birth date
Letter 3: The sixth letter of my birth month
Letter 4: The first letter of my birth date. Whew!

That was TIRING. You'll find my letter there, though.

Love,
S

All I can say is that both of you are mean.

Go ahead. Be friends. See if I care. I even thought of taking SRI LANKA's letter away, but I didn't do that because I'm not mean. Unlike you two.

The Wall Friends Club

4 July

Dear Ana,

I hope you figured it out!

You will always be my special wall friend, but I think we should allow the Other Person to be part of our gang. I love the idea of a gang. Don't you? And a gang must have more than two people. Our gang would be super-special, supercool! We could call ourselves the Wall Friends. Or the Wall Friends Club, or the Wall Friends Gang. What do you feel?

Love,
Sri

6 July

Dear Sri,

OMG, YOU ARE SO SMART! The clue was ... just so cool!

You're also very nice, S. I wanted to write you an angry note saying that I don't want to be friends with anyone else. I actually wrote all that, but then I tore it up because you're right. We should let the Other Person join. This is my last note for just you, tucked into the yellow bench, but I'm writing another one for the Wall Friends.

Your Anaconda

P.S. It was so smart to write 'seat' instead of 'bench'!

The Wall Friends Club

6 July

Hi,

We had a Wall Friends consultation and decided to include you in our gang. I am Anandi. WFA = Wall Friend Anandi. It is also Wall Friend Anaconda, but that is a joke you won't get.

I am almost ten years old.

The other founding member of the Wall Friends Club is Sriya, aka Sri Lanka. She is ten years old.

What is your name? How old are you?

As Sriya and I are the founding members, here are some rules:

1. **The Wall Friends Club is a secret club. You are not allowed to tell anyone else about us, unless we give you ~~perm~~ written permission.**

2. **You must write the date on each letter.**

That's all I can think of for now. We can add more rules later.

A

8 July

Dear Ana,

No letters yet! Do you think the other person, soon to be the next WF (hopefully), is upset? Were we very mean? (I hope not! I didn't want to be mean. But a code like that is like whispering in front of other people, isn't it?)

The Wall Friends Club

Love,
S

P.S. Sorry about the terrible handwriting. Writing this standing up so that I can slip it in right away.

---

10 July

Dear S,

Uh-oh. I hope not! The other person found your code mean, but it wasn't mean. You just wanted to get me to allow another letter writer into the gang. I was the one who didn't want anyone else to be part of this.

I feel a little guilty. So, if you're reading this letter, Other Person, I'm sorry.

I wish I'd been ready to include the new WF immediately because now I'm so excited about the idea of the Wall Friends Club! Maybe we could meet on special ocassions at a secret meeting place. Maybe we could solve mysteries. Or go on adventures!

But SL, I'm so scared that I'll blurt out something about the WFs that when I meet Veena, I sit quietly nowadays. And I'm usually such a chatterbox that she knows something is up and I think she's upset. What to do? I really don't like keeping secrets from my best friend.

Love,
Anandi

The Wall Friends Club

10 July

Anandi and Sriya,

Yes, I was upset. First with both of you and then only with Anandi. But this Other Person, as you called me, read all your letters. And left them there because I'M NOT MEAN.

I'll tell you just one thing about me, and you'll understand why I didn't write anything earlier. I am Veena. Yes, Anandi, your 'best friend' Veena.

11 July

Dear Veena,

Sorry, sorry, sorry. I'm so sorry, I was the one who asked Anandi not to tell you about me. I keep being mean without meaning to be mean. But I just really liked the idea of a secret friend. Anandi will tell you about my two best friends, so you will understand (I hope) why a special friend was so important to me. But then, just because I wanted a special friend, I made you and your best friend fight. I'm so sorry! I don't know what else to say. Anandi knows I like to fill up the paper so that I don't waste it, but I can't say anything more. I'm sorry, Veena. Will you be WFV?

Love,
Sriya

Apology accepted. 🙂 and now I'm just excited to be part of the WFC!

Love,
Veena

Uh-oh! I forgot rule 2 of the WFC—the date! It's the 12th of July.

---

12 July

Dear S and V,

Veena, oopsie. Sorry. But the good news is that I can now talk to you about Everything again!

AND I have the PERFECT thing for a club to do. There is a thief in my class!

So, here's what has been stolen so far:

1. Aarav's fancy scented eraser from China

2. Mishka's unicorn pencil

3. Our class scholar Vivaan's maths homework book

4. Two buns from Bani's lunch box

I have one very good guess already. I think the one who stole them:

The Wall Friends Club

1. Probably does not have any fancy stuff of his own
2. Was hungry

What does the WFC think?

Love,
Anachronistic

P.S. Our English teacher Mrs Rogers asks us to write a new word on the board every day to develop our vocabulary. I am the Vocabulary Monitor this week, so all the words I choose are going to begin with 'ana'! Veena, I'll tell you all about this letter game of ours and why the first letter you found was to Sri Lanka! I'm giggling as I write this.

---

13 July

Hello, A and S,

Anandi, what a fun name you have for this name game of yours! I don't know anything that begins with VEE. I even looked it up, but I found no words that I know, except ... VEENA. It's in the dictionary!

But hehehe, I just realized—aren't you glad my name does not start with S? Together, the Wall Friends Club would have been ASS! :D

A mystery is Awesome Fun. How cool it would be if WE solved it! I think your guess makes sense.

Yes. It must be someone who can't buy a fancy eraser or a unicorn pencil. My only question is, how are you sure the thief is a boy? It could be a girl, right?

The Wall Friends Club

Sriya, my father just came back from the US and he brought a bag full of chocolates, so this one's for you. Only one chocolate fits here in our gap at a time, so when this one's gone, I'll put another one in. I gave Anandi her chocolates yesterday.

Love,
Veena

P.S. Sorry, the letter is sticking out a bit. The wall is wet. It's a little gross to put my hand in!

---

15 July

All okay, Sri Lanka? The chocolate's gone, but you haven't written yet. Here's another chocolate from Veena.

Love,
A for Apple

---

18 July

Sorry, sorry, sorry, Wall Friends! All okay. First, I couldn't find any pamphlets and I really wanted to keep up the tradition of writing ONLY on the backs of pamphlets!

And then, all drama happened in school. Vee, did Ana tell you about my Enemy Urja? This is more about her.

The Wall Friends Club

Last Friday, Mrs Raj chose me as the new cupboard monitor. Urja didn't care. But then, on Monday and Tuesday, she saw how the teachers praised me for putting the key on a string and hanging it around my neck so that I wouldn't lose it. (It was my mother's idea, and she got me such lovely string and tied it so neatly. I was so proud of it!)

But this Urja! I hate her! On WEDNESDAY, she waited till Mrs Raj came, and only AFTER the teacher was in the room, she started CRYING! NOT UNTIL THEN! She made up a whole story about how no one ever trusted her with anything in her old school, and how she is so-o-o-o upset that it's the same in her new school, and how I get special treatment. Really? I get special treatment?

Finally, Mrs Raj asked me whether I would mind being the blackboard monitor instead so that the new girl would feel welcome. So I had to be the

25

The Wall Friends Club

'Bigger Person', as she always says, and hand over the key. Immediately, Urja's eyes were dry. Can you believe that? I mean, seriously.

It's not a big deal. Who wants to be the cupboard monitor anyway? But I don't like sneaky people.

My sister Kriya (yes, my parents gave us rhyming names) says I should just ignore them, but it isn't always easy.

Uff!

Anyway, back to the WFC. Veena, thank you so much for the chocolate! But ... I don't know how to say this politely in a letter ... I am not a big fan of chocolate. I took the first so that you would not feel bad, and I gave the second to Kriya, but please don't waste any more on me! Enjoy them and think of me when you eat them.

Coming to your mystery, Ana. I am not sure about your guess because I think any greedy person could have taken the stuff. The most important clue is the maths homework book. Does this person you suspect usually need help with maths? I think you don't have enough clues yet to find the thief. You can't look for footprints and fingerprints and all now since so many days have passed, but we need to ask some important questions. When were the stolen items last seen? Who remembers seeing them and where were they?

The Wall Friends Club

Ask the right questions, my co-detectives. Together, we will solve A Brand New Wall Friends Club Mystery!

Love,

Detective Sri

Whew! What a long letter.

---

19 July

Hi there, Wall Friends,

Urja seems like such a horrible person! We have a common enemy.

And you m–i–g–h–t be right, Sri, but I agree with Anandi. I think the thief is someone who can't buy things for herself or himself. A poor person, but remember—it doesn't have to be a boy! Any more clues, Ana?

Love,

Detective Veena

---

19 July

Hello WFC!

Veena, how, how, how, do you write so quickly? You're just too fast for me! It's as if you get a notification when someone puts a letter in the wall and then you write IMMEEDIATLY.

The Wall Friends Club

But yes, I do have more clues!

The reason I said 'he' or 'him' or whatever I said was that I suspected a particular person, someone who cannot afford to buy fancy stuff. Now, I feel a bit bad about having suspected him, and I'm glad I didn't tell anyone about my guess.

Basically, the peon's son is in our class, and I thought he might be the class thief. I know, I know, I shouldn't have jumped to conclusions, and now I know it was not him because we discovered another theft yesterday! Krish's history journal was stolen on Friday the 15th, and Venkat, the peon's son, was absent on Thursday and Friday! That's an important clue, right?

CLUE #1

But! There could be two thieves. Or more!

And! There were muddy shoeprints around Krish's desk. I copied the shoeprint. Notice how clear the shoe size is!

I felt like a super detective when I traced the shoeprint, but analysing it is silly. All of us wear the same school shoes. I asked ten children randomly, and NINE of them (including Krish!) wear size three, so no luck there. Any more ideas, detectives?

Love,
Anastasia

P.S. I'm a princess today!

The Wall Friends Club

20 July

Dear Girls,

I'm sad. Mrs Raj announced the results of the poetry competition. She said that my (our) poem was good, but it was not a 'kind' poem because it was not welcoming towards a new student. So we didn't win. Because it was not kind. If only I had changed that one name!

About the mystery—I'm glad you found more clues! The shoeprints are useless, I agree.

But I can't think of anything except the poetry competition results right now, so I can't help you today. Detective Sri is on leave.

Love,
Sad Sriya

---

21 July

Dear Sriya,

I'm sorry you didn't win the competition! Anandi told me about it.

Anandi, give us the latest scoop about the theft! We could write a book! Or a series of books! We could call it **Middle School Robbery: A Wall Friends Club Mystery.**

Love,
Veena

P.S. You spelt immediately wrong.

The Wall Friends Club

22 July

My dear Wall Friends,

I'm SOOOOO angry about the poetry competition too! Urja could be ANY Urja, right?

I did something Veena would do and I looked it up. Urja is a mineral water brand. Maybe THAT'S the Urja that doesn't know our secret. I'm so angry. AAAARGH!

And what about the other names, huh? Is there an Anandi in your class? And a Veena? I doubt it. But only Urja must be about the Urja in your class! I don't like your teacher.

The mystery at school makes me mega irritated too. No, Vee, we can't write a book about it. We can write one chapter. Max. You won't believe how the whole thing got solved.

Mishka's unicorn pencil was in her sister's bag.

Bani's bus friends stole her buns and fed them to the school dog.

Miss Thakur found Krish's history journal in the staff room.

Vivaan's maths homework book was with his tuition teacher—he forgot about it.

So, only Aarav's eraser is still missing, and that's not a real mystery, is it? I mean, EVERYONE loses erasers.

Case closed.

Love,
Angry Anandi

The Wall Friends Club

22 July

Your mystery became such a flop show, Ana! I was hoping for some excitement, some proper detective work. Now, it's just one big, fat phussss.

Love,
Veena

---

26 July

Tests today, so can't write much! All okay, S? I meet V regularly, but you haven't written for a bit!

Love,
Anandi, trying to be a scholar

---

27 July

Hi!

I didn't feel like writing for a few days, sorry. I got angry, Vee, that you could just write one sentence about the poetry competition and then carry on as if nothing was wrong.

But then I thought about how Mrs Raj keeps saying that we should not cry over spilt milk. No more poems for me! I'm better at puzzles.

Sriya

The Wall Friends Club

28 July

Sriya, I'm sorry you felt bad. ~~I you I think~~

Veena

---

30 July

Dear Girls,

Um ... this feels uncomfortable. Is the WFC fighting already? Please, let's not?

Love,
Anaconda

---

1 August

No, no, no, I don't want to fight either. I'm sorry, Veena! Maybe I just get upset too easily. Let's forget all about it.

Especially as this Sunday is Friendship Day! My classmates have all started making friendship bands. We do it under our desks, pinned to writing boards because we aren't allowed to make them in school. The teachers have confiscated I don't know how many so far! I'm sure they give them to their children to give their friends. What else would they do with so many friendship bands? At the assembly today, our principal made a long speech about how a single day to celebrate friendship makes no sense.

The Wall Friends Club

But WE can do something small and special, can't we?

Love,
S

---

2 August

Yes! We must do something special for Friendship Day! Ana, any ideas? You make the best friendship bands in the world!

Also, Sriya, if it upset you, it upset you. We had a workshop on bullying and that Bullying Aunty, I don't remember her name, told us that if people feel bad, we should step back and apologize without trying to justify ourselves, so that is what I tried to do. So, yes, I am sorry.

Love,
Vee

---

3 August

Dear WFC,

Veena, I KNOW you must get a notification when someone puts a letter in the wall. I KNOW it. You're just not telling us how.

And Sri Lanka, I think your principal and my principal wrote their Friendship Day speeches together.

BUT! Forget about teachers and principals and all. I have a STUPENDOE **STUPENDUS** plan for OUR bands. ~~I'm going to It's a secret!~~ I'm SO exited.

We now have the Perfect Reason for the Wall Friends Club to

The Wall Friends Club

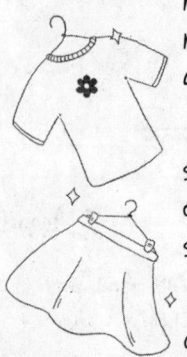

meet for the first time! Please, please, please, let's meet on Saturday, the 6th of August, at the wall! I'll give you my special surprise. Please?

And let's make this extra-special. Not small and special, Sri, BIG and special! Remember you said one of the things you love is new clothes? Wear something brand new for our first meeting!

Veena, can you do that too? Let's all wear new clothes! And will you get chips?

Sriya, can you get juice? We'll have a proper party!

Love,
A Very Exited Anaconda

3 August

Ooooh, I'm so curious about your special surprise!

Teachers are confiscating friendship bands in my school too. It's so silly. What's their problem?

But WE are going to celebrate it, and properly! Sorry, Ana, I won't wear new clothes because the park is mucky. I'll get chips, paper plates, tissues and sanitizer. Sriya, we'll need glasses too for juice, please! Ana, will you get Aunty's special cake? See you sooooon!

Love,
Veena

P.S. Anandi, stupendous is spelt like this, and EXITED is different from EXCITED. You aren't EXITING a room, are you?

The Wall Friends Club

5 August

Dearest Wall Friends,

I'm so, so sorry to be writing this so late. I won't be able to meet you tomorrow. (I'm writing this in school. Again.) My grandmother is ill and we're going to her house today. I hope you haven't already got the cake and chips and plates. If you have, please meet without me. I won't feel bad, promise!

Oh, and we have a mystery in my school too. But it's not so much fun because everyone thinks I am the thief. They haven't said so, but I see it when they look at me. The problem is that the things that have been stolen belong to my ex-friends. Esha's bottle, Sonia's hockey ball and Urja's pencil case are missing. Everyone thinks I stole them because I'm jealous. I don't know what to say when no one directly accuses me. They just whisper. And whispers are the worst.

Love,
Sriya

6 August

Hello, hi!

Hope your grandmother gets well soon, S!

And I'm angry that everyone thinks you stole the stuff! Do you have any clues? Can we make this our next WFC mystery?

The Wall Friends Club

I'm sad we can't meet today, but I understand. We'll find another special day to meet, don't worry. And Ana promises she'll secretly come and leave her special friendship bands for us here later today. I hope you can take yours!

Love,
V

6 August

Dearest Wall Friends,

Sri, I'm praying for your grandmother. I hope she gets well soon. We didn't meet without you. How could we do that when your grandmother is ill? But we will find an ocassion to celebrate very soon.

And that ocassion will be when your teachers prove that YOU ARE INOCCENT AND NOT A THIEF. I feel like coming to your school and shouting at everyone. How can they assume you are the thief just like that without any proof? Whispers are THE WORST.

Remember: The Wall Friends Club is with you!

It feels wrong to celebrate, but maybe my stupendous (yes, Veena, I learned how to spell it!) surprise will help cheer you up.

Here are your friendship bands! I took ages to make them because I had to plan each knot so that I could get WFA, WFS and WFV to be perfect! Yes, I made one for myself too! How could I not?

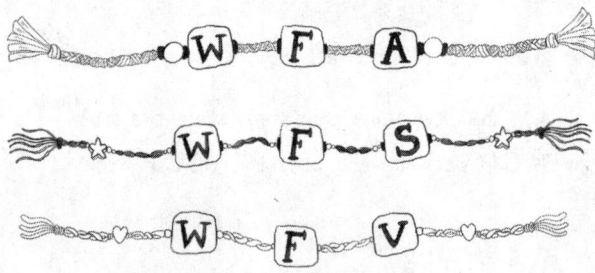

The Wall Friends Club

I am so glad I don't have a brother or sister who shares my room because I'm giggling as I write this because I imagined a whole conversation in my head.

It goes like this.

'WFA?' someone asks. 'What is WFA?'

'Why don't you guess?' I ask. (Smart or not?)

'Um ... Wall Flower Anandi? Window Falling Anandi? Writer Friend Anandi?'

And just like that, TANG! Lightbulb moment.

'Yes!' I say. 'Writer Friend Anandi. Two friends gave me this because they know I want to be the best writer in the world!'

What about you? What will you say?

Happiest Friendship Day to you!

Ana

6 August

Eek, Ana, this is the most special friendship band I've ever had! I've cleaned it properly so that there is no moss on it, and I will wear it all day tomorrow. But I want to wear it on Monday too! I'm going to hide it in my pocket when the teachers are around and wear it whenever they're not. I want everyone to see it.

If someone asks me what WFV stands for, I'm going to tell them it's a secret.

Or maybe I'll ask them to guess because secrets aren't always nice, are they?

The Wall Friends Club

Sriya, how is your grandmother? Does she live in another city? Are you back now and will you be visiting the Wall to take your friendship band?

Yes. We will celebrate on another OCCASION when we prove that you are INNOCENT.

Love,
Veena

P.S. Anandi, I hope you saw the hint. Here's a clue—it's about two more spellings.

---

8 August

Hello, hello! (One hello each, even though the whole letter is actually for Sriya)

Sriya, I'm still praying for you and your grandmother. I hope she gets completely well and that when we finally meet you, we can meet her too.

The friendship band is gone—you took it, didn't you? Please tell me you liked it! I made only four friendship bands this year. The fourth one was for a new friend in school. I'll tell you about her later. Maybe.

Tell me—did the real thief get caught?

Love,
Anandi the Anaconda

The Wall Friends Club

8 August

Hello, people!

What a special Friendship Day I had! I wore my WFV band all day yesterday and then today, it ALMOST got confiscated! Our English period was over, and we had our short break next, so of course I wanted to put on my friendship band and show everyone. I took it out and was just about to tie it, when Mrs Pereira walked back into class. She had left her specs on the table! I sit on the first bench, so I'm SURE she saw my band. But I did something super-smart. I dropped the band and quickly put my lunch bag on it. Mrs Pereira frowned and looked down, but she didn't say anything. Woooshhh! Saved by a whisker!

Another girl in my class, Sarita, gave me a friendship band too. I wore it when she was around so that she wouldn't feel bad, but I didn't wear it all day because I don't know if Sarita is very clean. Her hair is too oily and tied too tightly.

My parents told me I must give the maid's daughter a friendship band, so I gave her Sarita's band. Makes sense, right?

Sriya, please write soon!

Love,
WFV

The Wall Friends Club

9 August

Dearest Wall Friends,

I'm such a mixture of feelings today. If you put emotions into a bag and made that bag a person, that person would be me.

First, my grandmother is much better. So much better that she is making plans to go and see her brother for Rakshabandhan!

Secondly, I'm feeling a little weird saying this, but Veena, I feel you shouldn't have given Sarita's band away. I've chewed this pencil almost completely trying to see how I should write this, but basically, that's it. Why would you give away her friendship band because her hair is oily? It doesn't make sense, right? (Unless she gave everyone in class a friendship band. Then, the friendship band doesn't really mean anything.) But if she gave it to you because you are her special friend, I really don't think you should have given anyone that. I don't know Sarita, but it would make me upset if I found out that someone gave away my friendship band.

And even for your maid's daughter. Why didn't you just make a quick one for her? Wouldn't that have been nicer?

I'm sorry if this sounds mean and judge-y, but Mrs Raj keeps saying we should be brave and 'speak our minds'. I thought and thought and thought, and

The Wall Friends Club

then decided to write this. Sorry!

The mixed bag of feelings is even more mixed now because of the WFS friendship band. Anaconda, it's the best friendship band I've ever had. I wore it so proudly to school!

And they laughed at it. I heard them saying they were sure I made it for myself. I'm so, so angry! I couldn't say anything without telling them our secret, but I was FURIOUS, FUMING ... every single fancy word you can think of.

Worst of all is that there's no news about the thief and now there are more whispers about how 'deceitful' I am. Yes, I heard Urja use the word.

Finally, everyone laughed so much that I took it off and kept it in my pocket all day. It's now safe in my treasure box, where I keep all our letters and your picture, Ana, but why do people have to make happy moments so sad?

Love,
WFS

10 August

You have mean, mean classmates, Sriya! Why don't you complain to the teachers? Or ask your parents to change your school! Your

The Wall Friends Club

parents should go meet the principal. My parents would do that.

About Sarita—she doesn't know I gave her friendship band away, so it isn't mean, really, especially because I wore it all the time when she was around. I keep friendship bands from my friends, of course, but who can keep everything? She isn't at all my special friend. No way.

Love,
Vee

---

10 August

Dearest Sriya,

I don't know if I would be able to talk to the teachers. I am so scared of making a big fuss about what they may say is 'nothing'. Veena is much braver than I am! But I agree with her. You should talk to your teachers if you can. Tell them that your classmates are being mean to you. I do understand if you can't, though.

We're your friends, okay, S?

And I'm so happy your grandmother is better! I have another idea about when we could meet next, and I'll tell you very soon!

Love always,
Anandi

---

11 August

Dearest Wall Friends,

It's so lovely to have friends like you! I have excellent, excellent news. (But warning: this will be

The Wall Friends Club

a long letter!)

First, the backstory. Do you remember the cupboard monitor thing where I had to be the Bigger Person and give Urja the key? (Yes, this is about Urja. Again!) So. The new cupboard monitor will be selected tomorrow, and everyone knows Mrs Raj will choose me because I should have been the cupboard monitor last time.

Today, during form time, Mrs Raj asked Urja to open the cupboard for her.

'What do you want, Miss?' Urja asked.

'I just want to see what all we have in there,' Mrs Raj said.

And then, Urja started blabbering something and finally she said, 'Miss, I forgot the key at home.'

Mrs Raj frowned, but she did not get angry. She always says that people make mistakes, and that's okay. But she asked Vaishnavi (another girl in my class) to go and get the spare key from the staff room.

I don't know why, but I was watching Urja. I could see her getting panicky. Suddenly, she asked Mrs Raj if she could go to the toilet. We have form time at the end of the school day, so Mrs Raj told her she could wait ten minutes and then go. Honestly, it looked like Urja <u>couldn't wait!</u>

Vaishnavi came back and opened the cupboard. I was just watching Urja all the time. Her face was white.

The Wall Friends Club

Mrs Raj crouched to look at the bottom shelf and at the back ... what do you think she found???

1. Urja's 'stolen' pencil case
2. Esha's 'stolen' bottle
3. Sonia's 'stolen' hockey ball

'Why are these things here?' Mrs Raj asked.

And again, Urja started blabbering something. She didn't have any story planned, so she kept saying whatever came to her mouth. And then, finally, you won't believe what she said. She started crying (of course) and she said that she felt really, really bad about my poem where she was left out. She knew it was wrong, but she wanted me to be punished and she knew that on Friday I would get the key and she knew that I would not look at the bottom shelf immediately and ...

You get the picture.

First, I was angry. So, so angry. Enemy Urja was the thief and she wanted me to be blamed!

The Wall Friends Club

And then, I was SO relieved that the whole thing happened today. Urja was sent to the principal's office and she got a warning, but if they had found that I was the thief, my parents would have been called to school. I'm SURE of it.

Mrs Raj told everyone they needed to be careful with their things. That is the solution to <u>everything</u> for her.

I warned you it would be a long letter! Now I must RUN home!

Love,
Sriya

---

12 August

Oh my God, Sriya, what a letter! I don't even know what to say! I hate Urja. I'm so glad she got caught.

You know what it's time for? It's time to build the WFC and get more into the gang to support you and be true friends. I'm going to compose a proper letter. Coming soon!

Love,
Veena

The Wall Friends Club

13 August

Dearest Wall Friends,

Sriya, Sriya, I want to hug you! We WILL celebrate the fact that everyone found out that you are innocent. And we'll make it even more special because ... drumroll please ... we'll meet for the first time on my birthday! You remember I said in my last letter that I had an idea? This was the idea! I spoke to my parents about my birthday party, and I think it's perfect! What do you say?

I will leave an invitation card for you here in the wall, and you can come home for the party. Wouldn't that be the best celebration ever?

Love,
Anaconda

P.S. Vee, I have no idea what you mean by a 'proper' letter. Why are these letters improper?

Anandi refused to let me write my address on the letter, even though I told her what a proper letter is. She wants you to find out her address, and she's my neighbour, ONLY when she gives you an invitation card, and I was trying to write a formal letter because we're learning how to do that in school.

No more place for more explanations.

Sub: Building the Wall Friends Club

The Wall Friends Club

Dear Ms Sriya and Ms Anandi,

I am Veena Nair, a member of the reputable Wall Friends Club (WFC). I am writing to you to propose a new membership plan for the WFC. I suggest that we choose one friend each to become part of this exclusive club. In an earlier letter, Ms Anandi made a list of rules, which I seem to have misplaced. I request you to add those rules to the ones below.

    1. Every member must write at least one letter a week. Anyone who fails to do so will be removed from the Wall Friends Club.

    2. No adults must ever know about the WFC.

    3.

Kindly acknowledge receipt of this letter.

Yours faithfully,
Veena Nair
(VEENA NAIR)

Formal letters are so silly. What does 'kindly' even mean? There's nothing kind about receiving a letter. And if you look at the bottom of the letter, you know who's writing it. I mean, just look at the number of times I wrote my name there!

The Wall Friends Club

16 August

Dear Wall Friends Club,

No formal letter from me, sorry. Also, why would you write your address at the beginning? I don't understand. Do you write your real address in school? I don't want everyone to know where I live!

It reminds me of telegram writing, which one teacher taught us as a 'fun activity' last year. It was fun, maybe. But no one knows what a telegram is. Miss had prepared a ppt to explain, but there were no lights, so we never found out.

Anyway. More members? Sure! But I think the best number is five. You two could invite one friend each, and we'll reach the happy total of five. Perfect for a club, right? And rules? Hmm. Maybe we could just make them up later. I would love a password and a leader and all, but what's the point if we don't have a secret place to meet?

Ana, I would LOVE to come for your birthday party, but see whether your parents are okay with it, all right? We can just meet in the park someday.

Love,

Founding
An Excited WFC Member
(CODE NAME: Sri Lanka)

The Wall Friends Club

17 August

Dearest Wall Friends,

I have a new friend in school, whom I'd love to have as part of the WFC! She's the one I told you about—I made a friendship band for her this year.

We have a new project called Upcycle, and this girl Letty is going to be my partner. She is the Best Dancer I know, plus she's now my friend. She's a little shy and at first, so I thought she was unfriendly, but I was completely wrong. She's funny and friendly and lots of fun.

Anyway. This whole project is for an art exibition, and we'll sell what we make to raise money for charity! The idea of upcycle is kind of like recycle, but there's a difference. I didn't r-e-a-l-l-y understand what the difference is, but that's okay. What we're doing is more important, right?

My first thought was to use an old baked beans tin to make a pencil stand. The problem is that I don't have a baked beans tin, so I would have to buy one, eat the baked beans and then use the tin. That's cheating, right? It's not really trash. I'm making trash SO THAT I can use it. My other idea was to use a food delivery dabba as a pot in which to grow plants. Do you have a better idea?

Also, Sriya, why would only the two of us bring members in? Your classmates seem mean, mean, mean, but if there's someone in your building or colony who would like to be part of the WFC, or more importantly, whom <u>you</u> would like to be part of the WFC, invite them! Limited entry only, so choose well!

Love,
Founding Member Anandi
CODE NAME: Anaconda

The Wall Friends Club

P.S. Of course my parents will be okay with you coming for my birthday party! Why would they not be?

---

17 August

Ana, everyone makes or even buys trash to complete these projects. I did mine with ice-cream sticks last year, and you must be mad if you think I ate and collected so many ice-cream sticks! I just bought them at Kailash Stationers. The only thing I think is cheating is buying your whole project the way Kanu did. I mean, she just bought a bunch of newspaper bags and submitted them! Who does that?

Love,
Veena

---

18 August

Dear Wall Friends,

What is a baked beans tin? I agree with Veena. I don't think it is cheating because many children in my class buy ice-cream sticks and straws for these 'art from trash' projects. Nowadays, when we have a craft class like this, I just don't go to school because I don't see the point in buying trash to use for an upcycle project.

Using an old dabba as a pot is a good idea! Don't forget, you have to make a hole at the bottom.

Here are a few more ideas:

The Wall Friends Club

1. A bird feeder out of an old bottle
2. A patchwork dress or quilt
3. Do you eat eggs? You can make mosaic art with eggshells.
4. A rag doll

What do you think?

I'm trying to think of someone who would like to be part of the WFC, but I have no ideas yet!

Love,

WFS

P.S. I know a girl called Letty too, and she's a great dancer!

---

19 August

Hello!

You have such cool ideas, Sriya! I'm going to try and make a rag doll too, even though I don't have an Upcycle project in school! I found a video to help me.

What do you feel about one boy in the group? I have a friend

The Wall Friends Club

called Musab, who is my second-best friend. I would love to tell him about the WFC and bring him in! I know most other boys would not want to be part of a girl group, but he's cool that way. He doesn't care. He lives close by too, which is important, right? And he has a fancy five-bedroom house in Secret Alcove, can you believe that? What do you think?

Love,
Veena

---

24 August

Hello WFC,

Long time, no write!

Sorry, Sriya, you must have been wondering what happened to us. Or maybe not because it's so rainy. It rained so, so much that we couldn't come to the park. Do you know that it was the wettest week in decades? Veena told me that. She looked it up. Of course. We didn't have an official monsoon break, but for the first time EVER we had a holiday because so many roads were flooded. SURPRISE HOLIDAYS ARE THE BEST!

I feel bad for all the birds, though. I don't like pigeons, but the smaller ones look so sad! It's still raining, raining, raining, so I will go sploshing through the puddles to leave this letter for you. With the next letter, you can expect my invitation card. It has a special surprise, just for you! My parents are puzzled ~~by~~. No, I'm not telling you more. It's a surprise!

Love,
Anandi

The Wall Friends Club

26 August

Sriya!

We haven't heard from you forever! A's last letter was still there, still dry because she tucked it so deep in. What happened? Are you ill?

In both our schools, we have a fundraiser—collecting money for all those whose homes were destroyed because of the rain. Do you have something like that too? What are you doing?

Art exibition to the rescue! We're donating whatever we get from Upcycle to a place called Habitat, which makes houses for people who lose their homes because of natural disasters. I'm making rag dolls and bird feeders All The Time! I hope someone wants to buy them and that we manage to get some money.

My school is a bit boring that way. We don't have an EXHIBITION. The fundraiser is just a letter to our parents. We need to take however much money we like in an envelope with our name on it. That's it!

Write soon, S! We need to get our WFC going!

Love,
V & A

The Wall Friends Club

27 August

Dear Sri Lanka,

Here is my invitation card, as promised. It has Elsa on it, just for you! My parents were surprised because I've never LOVED-loved Elsa, but I insisted on an Elsa invitation card. Just for you.

I'm a little nervous leaving the card here, though. The old letters are ready to fall out. I'm pushing them deeper and deeper in, but my invitation card is still sticking out a bit. And it has my address on it, so I am scared of leaving it here. ~~My parents will~~ What to do? I want you to come, and how will you come if you don't have an address? I'm going to be ten years old, just like you, Sri. Two hands done, next I'll have to count on my toes!

But here I am chatterbox-ing-writerbox-ing away when really I'm just worried about my Wall Friend.

Please leave a note or something.

Love,

WFA

The Wall Friends Club

27 August

Dear Sriya,

We're worried about you, so I thought I'd do some detective work. Here are the clues I have:

1. You walk to school because you stay close by.

2. Your class teacher's name is Mrs Raj.

3. You are ten years old, so you are probably in the fifth standard.

4. In your class, there are girls called Sonia, Esha and Urja.

Here's what I am going to do:

1. I am going to search online and make a list of all the schools that are nearby.

2. I am going to talk to the other children in the society and find out who else goes to these schools.

3. I am going to find out what happened to you!

Don't worry. My case file is ready! It's the Third WFC Mystery: The Case Of The Missing ~~Wall Friend Sriya~~ Girl. Or The

The Wall Friends Club

Mystery Of The Missing Girl. I will find you!

Love,
Veena

---

28 August

Dearest Sriya,

The letters are gone! And on a Sunday! Please tell me you took them. I hope, hope, hope a wicked stranger did not find my invitation card. Should I have left it in the Other Place instead, the one you gave me clues for before Veena joined us? (I don't want to name the place in case the wicked person is reading this letter too.)

Veena and I are trying to solve the mystery, but we have not made much progress yet. We found one school that is really close by—do you go to Saraswati School for Girls? My mother said it does not have school buses and you said that Urja, Esha and Sonia take the school bus. So, unless Mamma is wrong about the school buses, you can't possibly go to Saraswati School, right?

But then, Veena says that according to her research, no other schools are walking distance from the park. Which made me wonder, how FAR do you walk really?

Please just leave a note or something. Please?

Love,
WFA/Anandi/Anaconda/Analysis/
(forgot the other word)

The Wall Friends Club

Houses Washed, Roads Submerged.

24 AUG

Several trees were uprooted and many houses collapsed in the incessant rain that ravaged the city on Monday and Tuesday. Nearly 450 people have been evacuated from their homes. Disaster management officials said that overflowing rivers had led to flooding in low-lying areas. No casualties have been reported. 'We had to rely on neighbours to rescue us,' said Prakash

---

30 August

Sriya?

Why did you leave a newspaper clipping for me/us? I told you about the floods, remember? I told you that we were doing a fundraiser for those whose houses got washed away ~~and~~

You confuse me.

It <u>IS</u> you, right? You are the one who left that newspaper clipping for me? Could you give me your phone number or something? I really

The Wall Friends Club

want to talk to you.

Love,
Anandi

Hi, this is Kriya. My sister would not rest until I promised to write a note for you and leave it here. Sriya was ill, but she is better now. She says she will write soon. She will not be coming for your birthday party, sorry!

---

31 August

Dear Kriya/Sriya,

Ana KNEW Sriya was ill even without my detective work. It's Ana's birthday today, so this letter is from both of us. We'll miss you at the party, S!

Love,
Anandi and Veena

---

2 September

Hello,

Detective Vee here. I think I solved the mystery. You go to Sungrace School, don't you?

Yesterday, my friend's cousin was talking about a Kriya who always comes first in class. I just thought I'd ask if she had a sister and aha!

Get well soon, S.

The Wall Friends Club

<del>Love,</del>
Yours faithfully,
Detective Vee

(Do detectives don't sign off with love? I don't think so.)

~~~~~~~~~~~~~~~~~~~~~~~~~~~~~~~

5 September

Dear S,

We miss you. The Wall Friends Club is no fun without you because Veena and I meet anyway. What's the point in exchanging letters?

You were right when you said you might lose your letter-writing friend if you came to see my dolphins. Veena and I never write to each other.

The dolphins are gone, by the way, because of all my birthday decorations. We put ten candles in each room! Veena wanted me to put balloons, but I don't use balloons because they're bad for the environment.

But everything was in tens. It was so special!

It would have been even more special if you had been there. Musab was here, so was Letty. But we didn't talk about the WFC, so I didn't ask her if she knew you.

Can we come and visit you?

My friends and I managed to collect so much money through our Upcycle project. It was amazing. We ran out of bird feeders and rag dolls, can you believe that? The people from Habitat came to thank us at the assembly today, but thank YOU, Sriya, it's all because of you and your ideas that we were able to collect so much money.

The Wall Friends Club

Get well soon. The Wall Friends Club needs you.

Love,
Ten-year-old Anaconda

7 September

Dear WFC,

I'm so, so sorry I disappeared. I was ill and there was no way to write. I'm going back to school again tomorrow. I can't believe I missed so much.

Good work, Detective Vee! I do go to Sungrace School.

And yes, Ana, I walk about two and a half kilometres to school. I know some people don't think that is close by. I will (hopefully!) start cycling to school soon. That will be so much faster!

Kriya told me she left a newspaper clipping for you just to tell you that someone took your letters. I think it was such a random thing to do. I mean, a newspaper clipping? Really? But she's the one who's going all the way to the park to leave this letter there for me, so I shouldn't be mean to her.

And yes, sorry, I had to tell her about the Wall Friends Club because I could not come for so long. I was so worried that you would think I had left the club or something.

I'm so nervous about school tomorrow. I know it is going to be just like my first day, when everyone will stay away from me because they will think I am

The Wall Friends Club

infectious or something. I am completely well now, but if I just cough or sneeze, even if I'm wearing a mask, everyone will step away. I just know they will.

Do write to me soon. I promise I will write back asap.

Love,
A Nervous Sri

---

8 September

Yay, Sriya! You're better!

And if you're fully recovered, I'm sure your classmates will just forget that you were ill. That's what happened to me when I got viral fever last year! I missed THREE WEEKS of school and everyone was just jealous that I was allowed to skip the first unit tests.

Oh, also, are you getting a new cycle? Geared? What colour? Ana and I love cycling!

Love,
V

The Wall Friends Club

8 September

Dear S,

I don't know anyone from Sungrace School. It's so wierd that we never told each other what school we go to, right? Veena is in L.K. Jain, and I go to Ridge View. You walk TWO AND A HALF KILOMETRES to school! Five kilometres a day! Wow!

Are you really totally, fully recovered? Did your parents drop you at school today so that you didn't have to walk so much?

Since we didn't meet on my birthday, I want to see when the next special OCCASION (happy, Veena?) is for us to meet. It has to be special! Don't you agree?

Love,
Anandi

9 September

Dear Wall Friends Club,

I knew what would happen in school yesterday. I knew it. They changed my place and asked me to sit at the back so that I don't infect anyone else. I don't even have a bench partner anymore. How come they didn't do that when Aryan fell ill? And Shubhangi? And Krishna? But no, if I fall ill, I get sent to the corner. Just so that I don't spread the infection.

Sonia and Esha now don't even talk to me anymore. They pretend that it is because I was ill and might spread whatever illness I have. Or they pretend that they are busy with hockey since they

The Wall Friends Club

are on the team, but I know.

Let me tell you the truth then because I am so upset.

1. You know when Urja said I had lice? It was true. I had lice. I was never so embarrassed in my life.

2. Would my parents drop me to school because I was ill? Are you mad? How would they drop me? By carrying me on their shoulders?

3. Am I getting a new, geared cycle? No. I'm getting my neighbour's old cycle, if we can afford it, and then afford to get it repaired. And even that is going to be only around Diwali.

4. Why did Kriya leave the clipping there? Because OUR house got washed away. The roof fell and the walls collapsed and we had nowhere to stay until we managed to build everything again. There was water everywhere. SO MANY people fell ill.

The Wall Friends Club

Does everything make sense to you now? There have been so many clues for you right through our letters. Why don't I have a photo at home? Why do I write on the back of pamphlets? Why can't I just change schools? Why can't my parents go and meet the principal? Maybe you can answer all those questions now.

Kriya has been telling me to be 'honest' with you from the time I told her about you. But what is there to be honest about? You tell me.

                                              Sriya

---

12 September

I knew it. I knew you would not want to be friends with me anymore once I told you everything about me. I am upset with you. I thought you were different.

But I was wrong and Kriya was right. I should have seen the signs, when Veena wrote about Sarita's friendship band. Is Sarita an RTE student like me? I could not stop thinking about my oily hair after that letter.

And you would never make a friendship band for your maid's daughter, right, Veena? Just pass one on, and might as well pass on one you don't like. My mother was a maid. I used to be ashamed. But now I'm ashamed of myself for not realizing what kinds of 'friends' I made.

I really thought I could make this last. But Musab

The Wall Friends Club

with five bedrooms will be a better friend.

Goodbye.

---

13 September

Sriya!

Don't give up on us! I was trying to find a way to give you something to show you I love you, my SL! And I was SURE that Veena would write because she's just so quick with these things. Remember, I said that I feel she gets a notification or something when someone puts a letter in the wall? I thought she'd write superfast, as usual. I wonder why she didn't write this time. I will talk to her about it soon. But I don't just want to be friends, S, I want to be BFFs.

I have something that I want to give you, and it's not going to fit in the gap in the wall. So, will you wait a tiny bit before I write the next letter, please? I'm not as smart as you are, so the code is taking a LONG time. And it's too wet for me to leave it under the yellow bench.

Love, always,
Anything You Want to Call Me

14th September

Your letter made me cry.

I can't stop thinking of all the letters I wrote to you. Did you never wonder why I never invited you home? I will. But I don't have a building and a colony.

I'll wait, Anandi. I just feel so lucky that I'm the

The Wall Friends Club

one who found your first letter that day.

Love,
SL

(I just realized ... those are REALLY my initials! My surname is Lokhande. Isn't that cooool?)

---

16 September

Dearest SL,

I don't know how to write this letter. I had a big, big fight with Veena yesterday. She didn't say that she doesn't want to write to you. She didn't say she doesn't want to be your friend. She didn't want to write because she knew 'you would feel bad'. I didn't understand at first. I'm sure you understand already because you're smart.

She said that she read in the paper that when streets are waterlogged, people get dengue and malaria, and how could we take the risk? She said that maybe it was not a good idea even in the beginning to write to a stranger. She said that we were not being 'hygeinic'. AND I DON'T CARE IF THAT'S NOT HOW IT'S SPELT. I want to shout at Veena, though, not you.

But really? We're hyginic when we play in the mud? We're hygenic when we drop a sweet and use the five-second rule? We're hygienic when we eat peru outside the park?

After that, at night, I thought of a thousand things to say to her. I got up at midnight and wrote them all down. I want to slip them into her mailbox. The only problem is that I don't want her parents to see the list before she does.

The Wall Friends Club

But that's that, Sri. The Wall Friends Club is back to being a two-member team. I'm sorry.

I'm angry and upset, and I can't imagine how you feel about it. I'm sorry. Sorry, sorry, sorry. How could Veena ever have been my best friend?

Love,
A

---

19 September

Dearest Anaconda,

I'm not surprised. I am sad, yes. But it has happened to me so many times that I cry and then leave it. I hate saying it so often but again, Kriya is right. The only thing we can do is to keep our noses glued to our books. Study well, keep studying and then, hopefully get good jobs and a house that does not wash away in the rain.

But I also think it is time for us to move our secret place. If Veena does not want to be friends with me, I don't want her to read our letters. So it's time for a new code. You have all the old letters, right, before she joined the club? You may need them.

Now, write down that vegetable which I love but you hate. And then, write down the first two lines of the original poem we wrote—the one that began with Urja, before we changed it. You have three lines of the poem, I know, but I remember just the first two.

The Wall Friends Club

(My box with all my letters got washed away. I'm sorry. Your favourite sharpener is gone. I promised to keep it safe forever. Will you forgive me?)

I'm sorry.

New place:

Word 1
Last word of the first line of the poem (easy!)

Word 2
Letter 1 — Last letter of the same word
Letter 2 & 3 — Last two letters of our Special Vegetable
Letter 4 — Last letter of our Special Vegetable

Word 3
Letter 1 — First letter of our Special Vegetable
Letter 2 — Second letter of Word 1 (from above, right here)
Letter 3 — First letter of the second word in our poem
Letters 4 & 5 — Third and fourth letters of our Special Vegetable
Letter 6 — Last letter of the second word of the second line of our poem (whew!)

Word 4
Letter 1 — Second letter of our Special Vegetable

The Wall Friends Club

(see how useful that vegetable of mine is!)
   Letter 2 — Second letter of Word 1
   Letter 3 — Same as Word 3 Letter 6

Word 5 (last word!)
Letter 1 — Poem Line 1, Word 4, first letter
Letter 2 — Last letter of our special vegetable
Letter 3 — Third letter of our special vegetable
Letter 4 — Same as Word 3 Letter 6
Letter 5 — Second letter of Word 1

Yay! I'm sure you'll get it.

Love,
Sriya

---

19 September

It was just so tiring to write that note that I have nothing else to say. But welcome to our new wall! I didn't want to use another bench because it's raining, of course, but also because we would not be the <u>Wall</u> Friends Club then, would we?

Love,
S

---

20 September

It's not fair. How are you so smart, Sriya? Just how? It isn't fair at all. I've been racking my brains for DAYS, trying to come up with some clue and find some place to give you the thing I want to give you, and just like that in one day you made this? How?

The Wall Friends Club

I can't possibly make up something even half as smart as your code, but I found something super. This gap is perfect for letters, but count three bricks down and four bricks left, and the brick there is loose. There's something special for you there!

I'll wait for you to see it and then I'll tell you about it.

I want you to know that Veena and I are not talking. I'm afraid of talking to Letty about the WFC because I don't want to get hurt again. I'll wait and find out more about her before I think about asking her to join.

Love,
Anandi Srinivas
(That's my full name, since I know yours.)

---

21 September

Dear Anaconda,

The diary you gave me is the most beautiful thing I have ever owned. I can never use it! How can I write in something that beautiful?

I didn't show it to anyone, and now I am terrified that Kriya will find it before I can find a private box and put my name on it. Your newest letters are inside my school calendar! I have to find a place to keep everything I own.

I've been sitting with this letter for half an hour, but I can't think of anything to say except more about Sungrace School and my classmates. I still sit alone at the back, even

The Wall Friends Club

though everyone knows that I don't have anything infectious. No one whispers about me anymore, but that is mostly because I am invisible. It would feel like a superpower if it didn't make me angry.

I don't want to write anything more about Sungrace. Give me some good news.

Love,
Sriya

---

21 September

Dear Anandi and Sriya,

I am sure you are still friends, but you must have found another place to exchange your letters.

I just wanted to say I'm sorry. I'm sorry about everything I said, and I'm sorry I stopped writing. ~~I was just shocked that Sriya had lice and~~ I have had lice too. Twice.

We hear so many things about diseases spread by water and waterlogging. I got scared.

I don't know what to say. And I don't know what to do.

Veena

---

22 September

Dearest Sriya,

Please don't reply to Veena's letter unless you want to. I thought of

The Wall Friends Club

taking the letter away so that you don't even have to see it, but then I realized you may have seen it already.

I don't talk to her even when I see her in the building. She may be sorry, but sorry doesn't change anything, does it? Everyone's been asking why we fought, even my parents. But I haven't told them anything. I won't. You'll always be my friend, Sri Lanka from the Wall. And if Veena writes again and you don't want to see it, just tell me. I'll quickly take it and BURN it.

No, sorry, I won't burn it. I'm not allowed to play with fire. But I'll tear it into small pieces and throw it in three different dustbins.

Let's not talk about Veena anymore.

I have something special for you in the little place where the loose brick was. I'm sure you'll like it. It's not good <u>NEWS</u> like you asked for, but it's a good something.

I've been talking to Letty a lot recently, and I really think she can be the next WF. I'll keep you updated.

Now tell me about you. Tell me about your home, your family, your everything.

Love,

Anandi

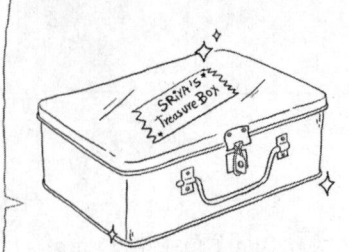

For my Wall Friend,
A new steel box for new treasures.

Love,
WFA

The Wall Friends Club

23 September

Dearest WFA,

I have so many things to say! Which is most important? Decisions, decisions. (Apparently there's a cartoon that says that. When Sonia was my best friend, she told me that.)

Okay, first. You are the kindest person I know. My Elsa diary and this new steel box are the prettiest things I own. I love them so much. But I must tell you something. Please, Ana, don't get me anything more. (Except on special occasions, maybe.) My father gets very angry when we get gifts, and our house is so small that he WILL find my things sooner or later. He says that rich people always think we need charity, and we don't.

(I know you weren't giving it to me as charity. You gave it to me as a gift. And I told you I love it. But.)

That's why I said 'no' to Veena's chocolates too. Remember? I love chocolate. I love chocolate so much that I could live on chocolate. But my father says that whenever people give gifts, they expect something in return someday. That's how it works. And I thought about it. I thought about how little

The Wall Friends Club

I knew Veena. If she called me home on her birthday, what would I give her? How can I keep taking gifts and not give anything back?

I know you understand.

Okay, second HUGELY exciting thing. I forgot all about Letty earlier, but Letty is short for Letitia, right? It HAS TO be the same Letty I know, Letitia Thomas! She lives in my basti. <u>I JUST</u> remembered that she got admission to Ridge View, and that's your school, right? We're not <u>friends,</u> but I know her and I like her. So yes, yes, yes, bring her into the WFC!

Finally, about Veena. I know Mrs Raj always says we should try to be the Bigger Person. But I'm fed up with being the bigger person. I don't want to talk to her, really. Sorry. I'm not even going to look at the old wall again. It makes me cry. If she writes a letter, you can take it, and don't tell me.

Love,
Sriya

25 September

Dear Sriya,

I understand about Veena. If I were you, I would never talk to her again either!

She keeps trying to be friends with me again, though. I just want to tell you, I m-i-g-h-t talk to her again soon because I feel very mean when I see her crying and all. But that's it. I'm not going to be friends

The Wall Friends Club

Letty/Letitia

or anything. And no way she's going to be my best friend ever again.

Letty IS Letitia Thomas, yes! I didn't know that. She always calls herself Letty, and, strangely, even the teachers call her Letty. So, I'm going to tell her about us tomorrow! I am so excited.

Love,
Anandi

---

26 September

Dear WFA,

I'm sorry I got overexcited and I asked Letty already. I think she's going to be an awesome member of WFC! She is nervous, though, because she says she makes lots of spelling and grammatical mistakes when she writes. I told her we don't care. Sorry, but I told her you make dozens of spelling mistakes too. I just wanted her to feel comfortable.

Yay, yay, yay! A new member, and one who knows us already.

So, just one thing remains. I want to meet you. We may not meet often. Maybe it's better if we don't meet often. ~~But will you come home?~~ I cut

The Wall Friends Club

that out and now I want to ask you again, will you come home? It's not a big house and we can't 'sit in my room and play' like all the children in school keep saying. I don't have a room. But I want you to come. Maybe you could even meet my parents and my grandmother. (Oh. That reminds me. My grandmother wasn't ill. That was a lie, and I'm sorry. But how could I tell you I can't get juice and glasses?)

Now, we don't even have to tell them about the WFC. I can just tell them that you're Letty's friend from school. What do you feel?

I want to meet you so much. Please say yes.

And yes, talk to Veena. I hope I can forgive her soon too. And maybe she'll be part of the WFC again someday. But not yet. First, I want to meet my dear friend Anaconda. When will you come?

Love,

Sriya

---

28 September

Dearest WFS,

I have a surprise for you. I'm not going to tell you what it is. But you will find out by the time you finish reading this letter. Don't cheat! Don't read the last line first!

The Wall Friends Club

I'm so glad you spoke to Letty. I met her in school, and it was like we had some sort of electric current running between us. I told her I would show her our secret wall in three days, max, because there were some small things that you and I wanted to do before bringing a new member in. She had so many questions!

Did you notice that when we started writing to each other, you had two best friends and I had one best friend, and now all three are gone? But both of us have one best friend now, who isn't going anywhere.

Maybe soon we'll have another best friend too. Let's wait and see.

But finally, it's time for the surprise.

I wish I could control the speed at which you read this. I want to meet you too. SO much. I thought and thought about the occasion on which we could meet. I want to come meet you at home. I want you to come home too. When? How? What occasion?

And then, I thought that meeting you itself would be an occasion. Right?

I found out what time school gets over for you. I thought I could be like Detective Sri because I know you walk through the park to go home. So I hid behind a tree, waiting to see who would go straight to the wall and take out a letter to read it. I hope you read it right here, or else it will all be a flop show.

Because there's a girl standing behind the slide waiting for you to turn around, and that girl is me.

Love,
Anandi

P.S. Can we hug?

The Wall Friends Club

Writing in Code

Uh-oh! Looks like someone else has found Anandi and Sriya's secret letter spot. The ever-resourceful Sriya has decided to create a code for the two of them to communicate without anyone snooping in. Here's how she did it!

The first step towards creating a code is agreeing on a language. Sriya picked English. Now, for every letter, pick a different letter. (But not randomly, otherwise you might have trouble cracking your own code!) Use a pattern—Sriya chose to change every letter to the one five letters ahead. For example, A became F, F became K, and so on.

So, this:

BMFY F SNHJ HTIJ!

became this:

WHAT A NICE CODE!

To solve it, you have to count back five letters from the ones written. This is called the key to a cipher. Anyone who has the key can solve the cipher. Ciphers can be anything from simple letter replacements to an entire system of beeps and boops, to something even more complicated. So go ahead, make your own cipher, and write a letter to your friend using it.

ACKNOWLEDGEMENTS

Dear Reader,

Have you ever received a letter? A proper letter?

I've received many, and I wouldn't have written this book if it weren't for all the letters I've exchanged right through my life. Pen pals I've never met, as well as my friends and family, made this book possible!

I think this is also a good time to tell you about the others who made this book with me. First, Tina Narang loved it enough to take it on, and then, Aparna Kapur edited it with me. She was such a joy to work with! She listened to what I had to say, and then nudged me in the right directions.

But do you ever just write without doodling? Don't you scribble in the margins? That's what Denise Antao did for this book, making it feel like a real set of letters. I love what she did!

You haven't met my family and friends, but believe me when I say that I wouldn't be a writer today if it weren't for them.

I'm also so glad you joined the Wall Friends Club as a very welcome guest. I hope you go on to write a letter (or many letters) of your own. Who knows? Maybe you'll find a letter-writing friend too!

Love,
Varsha

P.S. If you haven't figured it out already, I love letters. So please feel free to write to me! Unfortunately, email is now easier than a proper letter, but maybe you could write a letter, take a picture, and ask someone to email it to me at mail@varshaseshan.com

About the Author

Varsha Seshan is a Pune-based children's writer, with books published by Scholastic, Puffin, Duckbill, Young Zubaan, and more. She has been shortlisted for the AG-BLF Prize for Children's Fiction, the Neev Book Award, the Singapore Book Award, and the Scholastic Asian Book Award. As someone who loves silence, rain and the possibility of magic, she is happier with plants than with people. She conducts online book clubs and writing programmes for ages seven to 14 and is a classical dancer with over thirty years of training in Bharatanatyam. Find out more at www.varshaseshan.com

About the Illustrator

Denise Antao is an independent children's illustrator and graphic designer, currently living in Goa with her family and two dogs. Passionate about art and storytelling, she creates playful illustrations while exploring diverse themes and ideas. After completing her Bachelors in Design from Srishti Institute of Art Design and Technology, she went on to create illustrations for educational toys, games and now- books! She continues to grow her practice with childlike imagination and wonder.